Dear Parents:

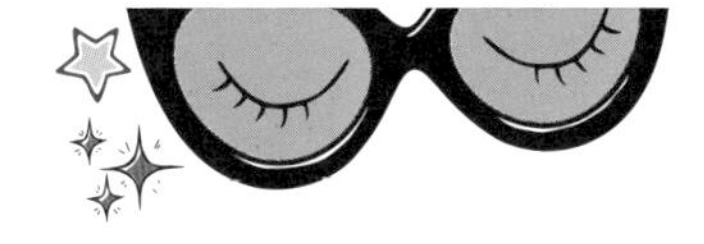

Congratulations! Your child is taking the first steps on an exciting journey. The destination? Independent reading!

STEP INTO READING® will help your child get there. The program offers five steps to reading success. Each step includes fun stories and colorful art or photographs. In addition to original fiction and books with favorite characters, there are Step into Reading Non-Fiction Readers, Phonics Readers and Boxed Sets, Sticker Readers, and Comic Readers—a complete literacy program with something to interest every child.

Learning to Read, Step by Step!

Ready to Read **Preschool–Kindergarten**
• big type and easy words • rhyme and rhythm • picture clues
For children who know the alphabet and are eager to begin reading.

Reading with Help **Preschool–Grade 1**
• basic vocabulary • short sentences • simple stories
For children who recognize familiar words and sound out new words with help.

Reading on Your Own **Grades 1–3**
• engaging characters • easy-to-follow plots • popular topics
For children who are ready to read on their own.

Reading Paragraphs **Grades 2–3**
• challenging vocabulary • short paragraphs • exciting stories
For newly independent readers who read simple sentences with confidence.

Ready for Chapters **Grades 2–4**
• chapters • longer paragraphs • full-color art
For children who want to take the plunge into chapter books but still like colorful pictures.

STEP INTO READING® is designed to give every child a successful reading experience. The grade levels are only guides; children will progress through the steps at their own speed, developing confidence in their reading.

Remember, a lifetime love of reading starts with a single step!

Published in the United States by Random House Children's Books, a division of Penguin Random House LLC, 1745 Broadway, New York, NY 10019, and in Canada by Penguin Random House Canada Limited, Toronto. The works in this collection were originally published separately in slightly different form by Random House Children's Books as *Let's Be Friends* in 2020, *Purr-fect Pets* in 2021, *The Kindness Club* in 2022, and *Be You!* in 2023.

Step into Reading, Random House, and the Random House colophon are registered trademarks of Penguin Random House LLC.

Visit us on the Web! rhcbooks.com

Educators and librarians, for a variety of teaching tools, visit us at RHTeachersLibrarians.com

ISBN 978-0-593-70974-0 (trade)

MANUFACTURED IN CHINA
10 9 8 7 6 5 4 3 2 1
Random House Children's Books Edition 2024

Random House Children's Books supports the First Amendment and celebrates the right to read.

4 Early Readers!

STEP INTO READING®

FUN-TASTIC TALES!

A Collection of Four Early Readers

Random House New York

© MGA
© MGA

CONTENTS

Let's Be Friends 7

Purr-fect Pets 37

The Kindness Club 67

Be You! 97

STEP 3 READING ON YOUR OWN

STEP INTO READING®

LET'S BE FRIENDS

by B.B. Arthur

Random House New York

Meet the outrageous members of the L.O.L. Surprise! squad! Life is always fierce and fun when you start a club with your best friends.

The Glitterati Club is full
of sparkly queens.
Queen Bee *bee*-lieves in herself.
She is swanky in black and gold.

Kitty Queen always lands on her feet.
Her kitty ears are the *purr*-fect accessory.

Sugar Queen is super sassy
and super sweet.
She adores glitter and always lives
the sweet life.

Boss Queen runs the world.
She is in charge
and always makes
it work.

Art is life for the Art Club.

Pop Heart draws bold lines.

She totally lives life in primary colors.

Splatters paints outside the lines.
She might make a mess,
but it will always be a work of art.

Every day is a costume party
in the Cosplay Club.
Bon Bon rocks pastel punk.
She thinks it is pretty sweet.

Neon QT always stands out.
She knows brighter is better.
When it comes to color,
she wants it all!

Glam Club does it up right.

But not all princesses

wear glass slippers.

Miss Punk was born to stand out

with edgy style.

Whatever As If Baby wants,

As If Baby gets.

She is totally a laugh and a half.

The Glee Club loves to sing.

Diva slays.

Rocker rocks.

MC Swag never drops the hot tunes.

ROCK ON
BABY
01
©MGA

In Opposites Club,

differences shine.

Fresh brings the chill.

Fancy brings the frill.

Fresh's style is street.

Fancy's style is sweet.

Yin and Yang
balance the scales.
When they are together,
they make perfect
harmony.

In Theater Club,
being a drama queen
is a good thing.
Merbaby is on her own wave.
She lives for the stage

©MGA

Only pop idols join the Pop Club.

Daring Diva is playing your song.

80s BB strikes a pose.

Oops Baby is lost in the game.

TOY

The Hip Hop Club
spins fresh beats.
DJ makes
the most amazing mixes.

Rock Club rocks out.
Punk Boi makes music
and mischief.

In Retro Club,

everything old is new.

Soul Babe is far out.

Go-Go Gurl is groovy.

STEM Club loves science.

VRQT is a super-smart tech guru.

She and PhD B.B. are always

on the cutting edge.

Sleepover Club

never forgets their pillows.

Snuggle Babe is a night owl

who dreams in black-and-white.

In Storybook Club,
stories come alive.
Bhaddie wants to hear the one
about the witch and her wicked ways.
BAD

In their totally cute clubs,
each fierce friend
does what she loves.
That is how they really shine . . .

SQUAD GOALS!
MISS PUNK

. . . and sparkle!

STEP 3 STEP INTO READING®
READING ON YOUR OWN

L.O.L. SURPRISE!™

PURR-FECT PETS

by B.B. Arthur

Random House New York

So many pets!

Pups! Cats!

Bunnies! Skunks?

No matter what kind you like,

these L.O.L. Surprise! pets

are off the leash!

MISS SKUNK

Queen Bee's puppy Pup Bee
likes to *bee* fierce.
She looks fetching
in her pom-poms.

Ruff Rocker is bad to the bone.

She helps Rocker rock.

Paws up,
Daring Diva!
Daring Doggie
is playing
your song.

Boss Pooch is a boss pup.
Boss Queen takes her
on power walks.

Fancy and Fresh

have *fur*-ever friends.

Fancy Haute Dog is cute.

She loves to be carried.

Fresh Feline is

Fresh's furry friend.

Who says cats and dogs

don't get along?

Kitty Queen and Kitty Kitty
rock kitty ears.

Not all cats hate water.

Merkitty loves to go to the beach with Merbaby.

Some pets are pocket-sized.
Splatters loves her skunk
with all her *art*.

Sugar Queen's pets
are small and sweet.
Sugar Squeak
is itsy-bitsy.

Sugar Sneak is
a teeny sweetie.

Punk Boi and Oops Baby
sing with their hamsters.

Punk Hog squeaks
against the machine.

Sometimes Oops Ham squeaks.
Sometimes she rolls.

80s B.B. has 80s babies.

80s Hog just wants to have fun.

80s Bunny is her

best bun *fur*-ever.

Pop Heart has an eye for art.

Hop Heart has an ear for art.

Soul Babe loves hip-hop.

Soul Bun does, too—

especially hop!

Some L.O.L. Surprise! pets
have stripes.
Diva, Miss Punk, and Snuggle Bae
love their skunk pets.
MISS PUNK

Diva Stripes thinks her stripes hypnotize.
Miss Skunk is a fuzzy punk princess.
Le Skunk Bébé thinks waking up stinks.
MISS SKUNK
CUDDLE BAE
©MGA

Some L.O.L. Surprise! pets have wings.
Unicorn's pony Unipony does.
She believes she can fly.

Bhaddie's monkey does, too.

Bhaddie Monkey knows she can fly.

Fly! Fly! Fly!

Go-Go Gurl's pet

is called Go-Go Birdie.

She flies on flower power.

Yin and Yang keep things Zen
with Yin Hoot and Yang Hop.
Everything is *owl* good
in their *hoppy* place.

Some L.O.L. Surprise! dolls
cannot decide
on just one pet.

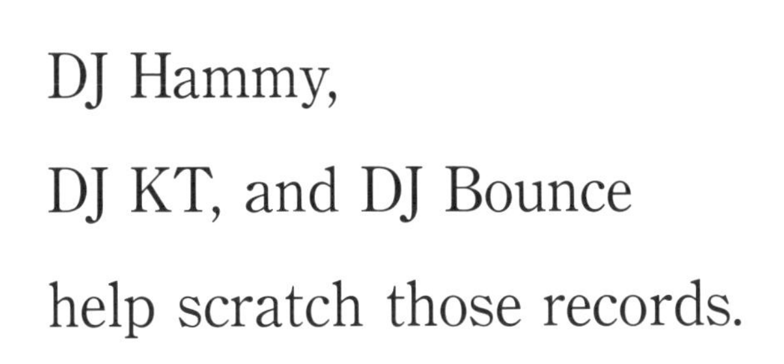

DJ Hammy,
DJ KT, and DJ Bounce
help scratch those records.

Bon Bon has all
the cutest critters.
These pets love
to dress up!
They are all
pretty in pastel.

Neon QT loves every color
and every pet.
Kitty, Hammy, Bunny, Puppy—
she wants them all!

These *paw*-some pets
know how to keep it fierce . . .

SO FIERCE!
©MGA

. . . and they are *purr*-fect pets!

STEP 3 READING ON YOUR OWN

STEP INTO READING®

THE KINDNESS CLUB

by B.B. Arthur

Random House New York

All the outrageous members
of the L.O.L. Surprise! squad
are friends.
Some friends are into fashion.
Some friends are into fame.
But all these friends agree
that the best friends are kind.

©MGA
©MGA

SHARING IS KIND

Surfer Babe shares her surfboard with Splash Queen.

She knows how much
her friend loves the waves.
The beach is always more fab
when you share it with someone.

TAKING TURNS IS KIND

MC Swag and Honey Bun take turns on the mic.

They pick out beats
for each other.
They love to hear
each other's rhymes.

INCLUDING OTHERS IS KIND

Dance Bot invites everyone to the dance floor.

More dancers mean more dancing!

Dance Bot knows dancing is the most fun with a crowd.

LISTENING IS KIND

Cosmic Queen wants to know
her friends' wildest dreams.

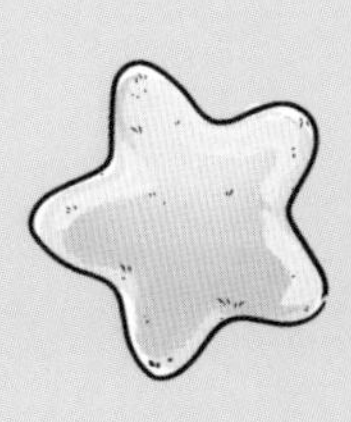

Soul Babe always listens
to her friends' deepest secrets.

Listening helps them learn
about each other.

HELPING IS KIND

Sometimes Instagold needs help getting connected! She wants to share her latest pic online.

VRQT is a tech whiz.

She helps Instagold in a snap.

SAYING NICE THINGS IS KIND

"You rock!" says Boss Queen.

"You rule!" says Rocker.

It feels fab to know
friends say nice things.

TOGETHER
©MGA

BEING PATIENT IS KIND

Drag Racer loves to go fast.

Flower Child likes to stop and smell the flowers.

It may take a little longer, but a friend is worth the wait.

ACCEPTING OTHERS IS KIND

It Baby likes to be fancy.

Grunge Grrrl likes to be casual.

Queen Bee loves
her curly, puffy hair.
Cosmic Queen loves her
rolls and curls.

They all tell
each other,
"I love your style!"

CHEERING FOR EACH OTHER IS KIND

When Supa Star is onstage,

her voice is powerful.

Hoops MVP

cheers for

her friend.

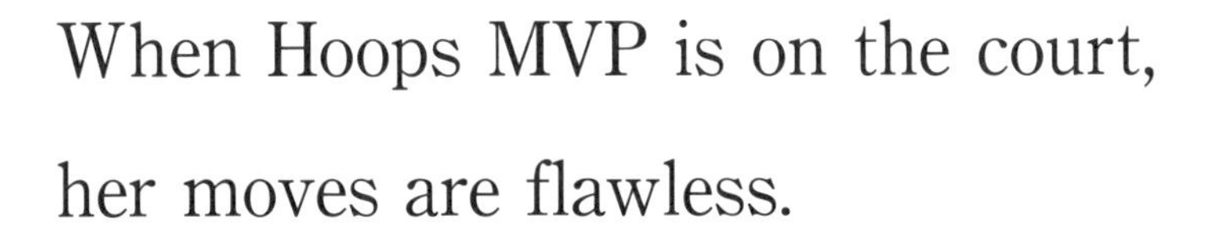

When Hoops MVP is on the court,
her moves are flawless.
Supa Star cheers for her friend
just as loudly in return.

WORKING TOGETHER IS KIND

Miss Baby loves pageants.

Miss Punk loves punk rock.

No matter how different they are, they agree that they love the stage.

KINDNESS FEELS GREAT!

Bon Bon feels extra sweet

when she is kind.

Neon QT feels extra bright
when someone is kind to her.

FRIENDS ARE KIND

Queen Bee is thankful

to have her squad around

her every day.

She feels lucky to have
such kind friends.

The L.O.L. Surprise! squad
love their clubs.
They have the glam club,
the glee club, and many more.
But in the end,
they are all in the same club—

BABY
01

the kindness club!

STEP 3 READING ON YOUR OWN

STEP INTO READING®

BE YOU!

by B.B. Arthur

Random House New York

In the L.O.L. Surprise squad,
everyone is different.
They love it!

Being different

makes them who they are.

Even when friends
are as different as
Yin and Yang,
they find balance—together.

Some friends want to wear
every bright color they can find.

Some prefer black and white.

Both Neon Q.T. and

Beatnik Babe rock their styles!

Some friends can be tough,

and some can be dainty.

Both Tough Guy
and Grand Queen
love to be themselves.

Some friends like to
rock out to metal.

Others love the twang of country.

Metal Babe and Twang agree that they both love music!

Some friends have short hair,
and some have long hair.

Crop it low,

or let it grow—

all hair is beautiful!

Curly, wavy, and straight hair,
pulled into a puff
or woven into braids—
every style is possible.
Every style is fab, too!

SHINE
BELIEVE
©MGA

This squad rocks
all skin tones.
They are all different,
and they all feel strong
in their skin.

©MGA

Friends have brown eyes,

blue eyes, green eyes—

every color!

Their eyes sparkle
like sequins when
they smile.

Some friends wear glasses.
Glasses may look fierce,
but they also help
these queens see
their fab friends.

Friends have

different hobbies.

Grow Grrrl likes to garden outside.

Tech Girl would rather be inside

on her computer.

Both believe in chasing

their passions!

Honey Bun likes a low-key style.

Her Majesty loves to be extra! These good friends stay true to themselves even though they are different.

Shiny Baybay likes sunny days.

Rain Q.T. likes rainy days.
Every person is different,
just like every day.

This squad can be as different
as punk and pop,
neon and pastel,
or fire and water.
But one thing stays the same. . . .

They are friends forever!
©MGA